One Night With My Dad's Boss: An Age Gap Instalove Erotic Romance

Willow Watkins

Published by Willow Watkins, 2024.

Table of Contents

Chapter One

Nathan:

"Hey," says a voice from beside me.

I turn towards it to find a semi-attractive woman, probably in her thirties, standing beside me with a smile plastered on her face. Her dark hair is piled up on her head in some kind of complicated style, and what should have been a pretty face is masked by several layers of makeup too many.

With a sigh, I lean back in my chair and take a sip of my drink, while giving her a polite nod. Unfortunately, she takes it as a sign to sit down beside me.

The bar is packed full tonight, and she could have chosen anyone. Yet here she is, bothering me. It's been a long damn week, and all I want is to have a couple of drinks to unwind on a Friday night. Is that too much to ask?

"I hope you didn't mind me coming over?" she asks, smiling and placing her hand on my forearm.

I grit my teeth to stop myself from yelling at her, and instead, work the corners of my lips up into a smile that I doubt looks at all friendly.

"Actually, I was just hoping to have a few drinks by myself tonight. It's been a rough week at work."

"What do you do?" she asks, fluttering her lashes at me and not taking the hint. "Wouldn't you much rather have someone to help drown your sorrows with? Or maybe have someone to help you work through that frustration in a much more physical way?"

Her eyes meet mine, and I feel her hand on my thigh, slowly gliding higher until I grab her wrist, stopping her ascent.

"I run my own IT consulting business," I tell her, my voice gruff and unwelcoming. "And I'm not interested. So run along and find someone else to throw yourself at."

The woman huffs and pulls her wrist out of my hand before storming away.

Thank god for that.

I let out a breath and take another sip of my drink. You'd think that after all this time, I would be desperate for a woman's attention. But I haven't met anybody I've wanted to have sex with for a very long time.

Not since my ex-wife ran away with the guy who was supposed to be my best friend ten years ago. Apparently, that was enough to put me off women for life. So ever since then, I've been focused on building my business, and I've done very well for myself.

That's all I need in life.

My eyes roam across the dance floor, and this time, my smile is more genuine. I've always been a people watcher, and seeing so many people let their hair down and have fun makes me happy. Of course, their drunken shenanigans are fun to watch too. These young kids who can't hold their liquor are prone to doing stupid things, just like I was at their age.

A young woman catches my eye. She's dancing with a couple of other women about the same age, but there's something different about her. There's a smile on her face that makes my heart stop.

Her long blonde hair is curled in loose waves and it hangs halfway down her back. She's wearing a dress that ends just above her knees and shows off a toned pair of legs that any woman would be jealous of, and when she throws her head back, laughing at something her friend says, I feel it.

She's beautiful, but that's not what makes me stop and stare. The way her whole face lights up when she smiles, the way her body moves with such fluidity and grace... It makes my dick twitch and has me thinking all kinds of dirty thoughts.

But it's her eyes that are her best feature. When she stops dancing and they land on mine, I feel as if an electric current is flowing between us.

I don't know how long we stare at each other, but eventually she looks away. I can't stop watching her, though, even when her eyes drift back to mine every so often.

She's a fucking goddess, and I'm not sure she even realizes it.

A couple of men come over and start dancing with the group, but she keeps looking at me, and I can't resist. I finish the rest of my drink and get to my feet, making my way through the crowd towards her.

When I'm right behind her, I place my hand on her arm, and her head snaps up. Her blue eyes are wide and questioning as she looks at me.

"Do you want to dance?" I ask, not giving her a chance to respond before pulling her towards me.

She giggles and wraps her arms around my neck, moving her body closer to mine. We start dancing, and I feel my dick grow hard.

"I'm Nathan," I say, dipping my head to speak directly into her ear so she can hear me over the music. "What's your name?"

"I'm Emily," she says, her cheeks flushed.

I move closer, and she gasps when she feels my erection press against her. Her eyes lock on mine, and she bites her lower lip.

I want her.

It's crazy to feel this way about someone so quickly, especially when the only thing I know about her is her name. But there's something about her that draws me in.

Her lips are full and inviting, and I have a sudden urge to kiss her. To taste her. But I hold back. For now.

I move my hand to her hip and pull her even closer, feeling her breasts brush against my chest. Her eyes widen, and she licks her lips.

"How would you feel if I told you that you'll be spending the night with me, Emily?" I ask her, unable to keep the growl out of my voice.

She blushes and ducks her head, but not before I see the smile tugging at her lips.

I know I'm pushing my luck. I'm a forty-nine-year-old who hasn't had a relationship in a decade, while she can't be any older than her mid-twenties, and I have no doubt she could get any man in this club. But I've built an incredibly successful business by pushing my luck, and maybe it's time to start looking for a similar kind of success in my personal life.

"I'd feel lucky to be the one you choose," she says in a voice so soft I have to strain to hear it.

Her answer sends a surge of desire coursing through me, and I tighten my grip on her. I know I'm playing with fire, but I don't care. I've never wanted a woman more than I want her right now.

"Is that so?" I ask, moving my hand up to her chin and gently tilting her head up towards me.

She nods, and her gaze darts down to my lips before returning to my eyes. "Although I'm not sure how my friends will feel if I just leave them stranded here while we're out celebrating my birthday. I was supposed to be staying over with them tonight."

"It's your birthday?" I ask, raising an eyebrow.

The corners of her pretty pink lips tug upwards into a smile that makes my cock ache with need.

"My birthday was yesterday, but we waited until Friday night to celebrate. I just turned twenty-one."

I have to hold back a groan. She looks a little older than that, so it's a surprise to hear she's so young. I should probably back off and let her find a guy her own age.

But I don't want to.

I want to take her somewhere more private and show her what a real man can do.

"Well then, I guess I should help make your birthday one to remember," I say, pressing my hips forward so she can feel the effect she has on me.

She sucks in a sharp breath and her eyes widen, but she doesn't pull away. In fact, as we sway in time to the music, she seems to rub herself against me even more.

The sexy little minx.

Unable to resist any longer, I lean down to claim her lips. They're soft and supple, and I can taste the sweetness of her strawberry lip gloss. I deepen the kiss, exploring her mouth with my tongue and swallowing her soft moan.

She kisses me back with just as much fervor as I feel, and she runs her fingers through the hair at the nape of my neck to send a shiver down my spine.

The music fades away as we lose ourselves in each other, and the rest of the world disappears. It's just me and her, and the heat of our desire.

Eventually, I have to pull away for air, and her eyes flutter open. She stares at me with a look of awe on her face, and her lips are slightly swollen from our passionate kiss.

Fuck. If this is how good she looks after just one kiss, I can't wait to see how she looks when she's screaming my name during one of the many orgasms I plan to give her tonight.

"What do you say we get out of here?" I ask, running my thumb across her lower lip. "There's a hotel just down the road we can go to. I'll pay, of course."

Her tongue darts out to brush against the digit, and I almost moan. It puts all kinds of images in my mind of Emily on her knees, using that tongue on my dick.

"Sounds good," she says in a breathy voice. "I just need to tell my friends where I'll be going, then we can leave."

I nod and very reluctantly release my hold on her. It will only be for a few minutes, then I'll be able to hold her all night.

She moves over to her friends, who are looking at me with curiosity, but my attention is firmly fixed on Emily. I can't wait to get her alone and find out how good she tastes, and how loud she screams when she comes.

When Emily turns back to me with a bright smile on her face, I start to suspect that just one night with her won't be enough for me.

I have a feeling I'll be keeping her.

Chapter Two

Emily:

Nathan is hot.

He's got these gorgeous hazel eyes that seem to see right through me, and this rugged jawline with a five o'clock shadow. Not to mention the salt and pepper hair that has me weak at the knees. He looks like the kind of man who knows exactly what he's doing, and the thought of having his hands all over me makes me wet.

As we walk down the street to the hotel, I'm very aware of the fact that I'm practically skipping. This is going to be my first time, and it's going to happen on my twenty-first birthday. Almost. It's like the stars aligned to bring Nathan and me together at the perfect time.

My friends have always teased me about waiting so long to give my virginity away. But the truth is that I've been waiting for someone special. Someone who makes me feel tingly and hot all over from the very first moment we meet, just like all the characters in the romance books I love to read.

If it's not love at first sight, I don't want it.

Sure, I've been out on a few dates in the past, and I've even made out with a couple of them, but none of them created the kind of spark inside me that Nathan did as we'd gazed at each other across the dance floor tonight. The way he'd watched me dancing with my friends with such an intense look on his face, never once taking his eyes off me, had given me goosebumps.

So, when he'd come up and asked me to dance, I'd jumped at the opportunity. And as soon as his arms had wrapped around me, I knew that I wanted him to be the one. Every small touch had sent little jolts of pleasure through my body; and if he's able to make me feel that way when we're dancing, I can only imagine how good it will feel when we are alone and naked.

He places a hand on the small of my back and guides me through the door of the hotel as he holds it open for us.

My jaw drops as soon as we enter. This place is nice. Way nicer than anything I could ever be able to afford on my minimum wage salary from the animal shelter. But I love my job there, so it's not like I want to find a better-paying job. For now, I'm happy knowing that I'm doing something small to help the animals who have been abandoned.

Nathan strides up to the receptionist's desk, and she greets him with a wide smile. "Welcome to the Park View Hotel, Sir. How can I help you today?"

"I'd like to book a room for the night," he says, his voice smooth and confident.

The receptionist glances at me and then back at him, and I can see the questions in her eyes. After all, he looks old enough to be my father. Not that I mind that at all. He looks sexier than any guy my own age that I've ever met.

"Of course, Sir. If you'd just fill out this form for me and provide a credit card, I'll get a room sorted for you."

He nods and quickly fills out the form before sliding it back to her. Is it wrong that I find it so damn intriguing that he can afford a room in this place seemingly without having to give it a second thought?

The woman takes a keycard out of a box on her desk and passes it to him, and he grabs my hand and pulls me towards the elevator.

As soon as the doors close, he spins me around and presses me against the wall. His lips crash down onto mine, and I moan as his tongue darts into my mouth, exploring and tasting. He grips my waist and lifts me up, and I wrap my legs around his hips, pressing myself closer to him.

The bulge in his pants brushes against the most intimate part of me, and I feel my arousal grow.

I've never felt this way before, and it's intoxicating.

I grind against him, and he groans, biting down on my lower lip and eliciting a soft gasp from me.

"Fuck, you're sexy," he murmurs against my lips.

The elevator pings, signaling that we've arrived at our floor, and Nathan places me back down, letting out a frustrated little sound that makes me grin.

As soon as we step out, he grabs my hand and practically drags me along behind him. He's clearly impatient to get into the room, and honestly, so am I. I'm aching with need, and I want nothing more than for him to rip my clothes off and show me everything I've been missing out on so far.

When we reach the door, he swipes the key card and pushes the door open, pulling me into the room.

The second the door closes, his lips are on mine again, and his hands are roaming all over my body.

His touch feels amazing, and I moan softly.

I move my hands up his chest, enjoying the feeling of the hard muscles underneath the thin fabric of his shirt.

"You're overdressed," he says in a husky voice.

Before I can respond, his hands are on the zipper of my dress. He pulls it down slowly, and his eyes are fixed on mine the whole time.

When he reaches the bottom, the dress falls away, and I'm left standing in front of him in just my bra and panties.

I blush and duck my head, feeling exposed under his gaze.

"Don't be shy, Emily. You're fucking gorgeous."

His words send a thrill through me, and I look up at him.

He's still fully clothed, and I'm dying to see him without his shirt.

I move my hands up his chest again, slowly undoing the buttons and revealing a muscular chest and abs.

God, he's perfect.

When his shirt is open, I slide it down his arms and drop it to the floor.

I run my hands over his bare torso, and his muscles tense under my touch. Unable to resist, I lean closer and begin peppering his chest with gentle kisses, enjoying the little grunts that emerge from him with each one.

While I'm focused on him, he reaches behind me and unclasps my bra, before pushing it to the floor and cupping my breasts in his hands. He rolls my nipples between his fingers, and I moan as a bolt of pleasure shoots straight to my core.

"Nathan," I gasp, throwing my head back and closing my eyes.

He doesn't reply, instead he leans down and captures one of my nipples in his mouth. He swirls his tongue around the hardened peak and sucks it gently.

I gasp and thread my fingers through his hair, holding him in place.

He releases my nipple and gives it a final lick before moving to the other and giving it the same attention.

It feels so good, and my panties are soaked with desire.

I need him, and I need him now.

"Nathan, please," I whimper, tugging at his hair.

He pulls back and smirks. "Please, what? What do you want, Emily?"

I take his hand and press it between my legs. He chuckles and slips a finger inside my panties. He traces my slit, teasing me before plunging a finger inside.

"Oh god," I moan, as he curls his finger and hits just the right spot.

"You're so fucking wet," he groans, his eyes locked on mine.

He adds a second finger and starts pumping in and out of me.

"You're so tight, babygirl. I can't wait to feel you wrapped around my cock."

I shudder, and he pulls his fingers out. A frustrated groan escapes me, but he just grins and licks my juices off them.

"I need to be inside you, Emily,"

"Yes, please," I beg.

He pulls his pants and boxers off, revealing his hard cock. He strokes himself, and I watch, mesmerized. He's big, bigger than I expected, and I'm not sure how he's going to fit inside me.

But before I can worry too much, he lifts me in his arms and carries me over to the bed, placing me down gently on it.

His fingers hook into the waistband of my panties and he slides them down my legs, leaving me completely bare to his gaze. The way he looks down at me creates a warm feeling in my chest, and an inferno between my thighs.

"Open your legs for me, babygirl," he commands, while he grips his cock in his hand and begins casually stroking it. "Show me what is mine for the night."

I bite my lower lip as I comply with his demand, spreading my legs open and giving him an eyeful. He growls, a sound so primal and raw that I swear my pussy clenches, and he steps forward, climbing onto the bed and lowering himself down on top of me to settle between my parted thighs.

He lines his cock up at my entrance, and his other hand tangles in my hair, tilting my head back and forcing me to look into his eyes.

"Last chance, Emily," he rumbles. "Are you sure you want to do this?"

"I'm sure," I whisper, staring into his eyes. "I need this so badly, Nathan."

And it's the truth. Every fiber of my being is buzzing with the need for him to be inside me. For a moment, I consider telling him that he will be my first, but then a worry claws at my insides.

What if he decides he doesn't want someone so inexperienced? What if he just laughs at me and leaves?

I don't want that, so I keep quiet and wriggle beneath him, making my pussy rub shamelessly against the swollen head of his erection.

He growls again and pushes forward, sliding his cock inside me inch by glorious inch. It stings a little as he stretches me wide, but when he brings a hand up to toy with a sensitive nipple, the pleasure of his touch mingles with the sting in the most delicious way.

"More," I gasp, clawing at his back as I wrap my legs around his hips.

"Such a greedy girl," he growls, sinking the last few inches of his cock into me. "So tight. So fucking perfect."

He pulls back, nearly withdrawing entirely, and then slams back in. He repeats the motion a few times, each time picking up the pace until his thrusts are powerful and deep, sending jolts of pleasure through me.

"Yes, Nathan!" I cry out, digging my nails into his back and clinging onto him like my life depends on it.

The bed shakes with the force of his thrusts, and the sound of flesh slapping together fills the air; but I'm too lost in the pleasure to care.

It's better than anything I could have imagined, and I never want it to stop. Even though I know I'm going to be very sore once he's finished with me.

"That's it, babygirl. Take my cock," he rasps, burying his face in the crook of my neck and sucking on the sensitive skin there.

"Fuck, Nathan!"

"Are you gonna come for me?" he growls, biting down on the sensitive flesh and sending a new wave of pleasure through me. "Are you gonna come on my cock, babygirl?"

"Yes!" I scream, arching my back and clawing at his shoulders as my orgasm crashes over me.

My pussy clenches around his cock as the waves of pleasure wash over me, and he groans, his thrusts becoming erratic while he chases his own release.

"Fuck, babygirl, I'm gonna come," he growls, and with one final thrust, he spills himself inside me.

We lie together, breathing heavily as we come down from our highs. And when he finally rolls off me, he pulls me into his arms and holds me tight.

"That was incredible," I whisper, curling into his side and resting my head on his chest.

"Yeah, it was," he agrees, pressing a kiss to the top of my head. "You were perfect."

I smile and close my eyes, basking in the afterglow of our lovemaking.

He runs his fingers through my hair, and I sigh happily. This is exactly how I pictured my first time going, and it's everything I could have hoped for.

Chapter Three

Emily:

"Are you sure you're okay, Emily?" Mom asks for probably the millionth time today.

"Yes, Mom," I snap. "I'm fine."

But that isn't the truth. Far from it. I'd woken up at five this morning in the arms of a complete stranger and filled with shame that I'd given in so easily to my childish romantic notions. I'd given away my virginity to someone without a second thought, and there's no way I can get it back now.

Sure, it had been amazing. Mind-blowing, even. But I still feel stupid for rushing into it. I'm twenty-one. An adult. And I shouldn't be making those kinds of impulsive decisions anymore.

The shame I'd felt when I'd woken up had been so great that I ended up sneaking out of the hotel room before Nathan had even woken up. Which has turned out to be another impulsive decision I've come to regret. I don't know anything about him except his first name, and even if I wanted to get to know him better, I can't now.

It's not even as if I can blame my foolishness on alcohol, seeing as I'd been stone-cold sober when I'd met him. But I wish I had that excuse so I wouldn't have to feel so stupid about the whole thing today.

Oh well, at least tonight might be a good opportunity to get Nathan out of my mind.

I'm in the car with my mom and dad, heading to a party being thrown by Dad's boss. It's some kind of celebration for the big uptick in profits this year, I think. I'm not even really sure what my dad does, except that it's something to do with technology. Whenever he talks about work, my brain automatically switches off. So I can only imagine how boring his boss must be.

This party isn't really my kind of thing, but my parents insisted, and I was getting tired of moping around the house after last night. So at the last minute, I'd decided to stop resisting and just go to the damn event.

I just have to hope this impulsive decision isn't followed by even more regret.

Dad turns onto a driveway, which seems to go on forever, before a huge house appears from behind all the trees lining the road. It's beautiful, with a sprawling garden and a huge water feature out front.

It looks like the sort of place where rich, old, white men get together and make big business deals. Why am I not surprised that Dad's stuffy old boss lives in a place like this?

He finds a spot to park along the side of the driveway, which is crowded with cars by now, and then turns in his seat to face me.

"Now, Emily, when you meet Mr. Harding, I want you to just smile and nod at everything he says, okay? He's an incredibly smart and powerful man, and after the year I've had at work, I'm hoping to be promoted to a senior management position, so you need to be on your best behavior."

I resist the urge to roll my eyes, but only just. Sure, I'm his daughter, but I'm not a damn toddler. What the hell does he think I'm going to get up to at this party?

"Sure, Dad. I'll behave like an angel, okay?"

He lets out a sigh and turns back around, getting out of the car. Mom and I exchange a knowing look and get out as well. She squeezes my arm, and I smile. At least my mom understands that Dad can be a little much sometimes.

The three of us head towards the large house, and we're greeted by some guy in butler livery who's holding a tray filled with glasses of champagne for the new arrivals. Mom and Dad both take one and stop to make small talk with another couple hanging out at the front of the house, while I walk in and begin looking around.

There are already a lot of people here, and I can hear a live band playing somewhere in the distance. It sounds like jazz music, which is not my thing. But I'm here to support my parents, so it's not like I was expecting to have an amazing time, anyway. I'm just here to keep myself distracted.

The house looks even bigger from the inside. It's a mansion, really, and I wonder just how many rooms it has. Maybe I can sneak off to explore after a bit. If nothing else, it would be a way to escape all the small talk with old men that Dad is probably going to try and put me through tonight. It's Mom's job to stand politely at his side while she's bored out of her mind. Not mine.

I move further into the house, finding a large room that's crowded with people. The music is louder here, and there are several couples dancing in the center of the room. Everyone seems to be wearing their fanciest clothes, and I realize that I probably should have made a bit more effort.

My dress is pretty, but it's not exactly what I'd call a formal party gown. Oh well. It's too late now, and no one's even looking at me, anyway.

Before I can set foot into the room, though, a large hand grabs my wrist and pulls me away, tugging me down a dark corridor.

"Hey!" I screech. "What the hell do you think you're doing?"

The man pulling me away from the party is wearing a tux that I know had to have cost an insane amount of money. There is something familiar about him, but as he pulls me along, I can only see his broad shoulders and the back of his head, so I can't figure out who it is.

Suddenly, I find myself being pushed back against the wall, the imposing man trapping me there with one hand on the wall either side of my body. My gaze travels upwards to find his face, and I let out a gasp.

"Nathan!"

His lips curl up into a smirk, and a rush of butterflies appears in my stomach.

"I bet you weren't expecting to see me here tonight," he says, his eyes roaming down over my body as if he wants to devour me. "Although, I have to say, I wasn't expecting to see you either. Who are you here with?"

"M...my dad," I stutter nervously.

Somehow, Nathan seems even better looking today, and his body in that suit is doing things to me that I can't explain.

"And who's your dad?"

"Ted Walker," I tell him, and his eyebrows shoot up in surprise.

"So you're Ted's daughter?" He chuckles, the sound so deep and gravelly it's almost a growl. "Well, aren't you a naughty girl?"

He moves his hand down from the wall and cups my cheek. He strokes his thumb along my lower lip, and I'm frozen in place, unable to think straight, let alone move.

"You know my dad?" I ask after I finally regain some of my senses.

It takes a moment for Nathan to process the question, as he remains seemingly fixated on my lips. Oh god, is he going to kiss me? Should I even want him to? So many emotions are swirling around inside of me, but the most prominent one is the desire to press my lips to his.

"Of course," he finally replies, tearing his gaze away from my mouth to look into my eyes. "Ted is one of my many employees."

"You're the boss?" I squeak, my heart pounding in my chest.

I feel a sudden rush of panic and embarrassment as I try to make sense of what he's saying.

Oh no. Did I fuck my dad's boss last night? This whole thing is messier than I ever realized.

"The boss, the CEO, the owner." He smirks. "I'm all of those things."

My mind is a complete mess. I feel sick, and dizzy, and confused, and... oh god. He's leaning in, and his lips are on mine, and I'm melting. His kiss is hard and hungry, and his hand curls around the back of my neck, holding me in place.

My hands move to his chest, and I can feel the hard muscle underneath the expensive fabric of his tux.

"We can't do this," I gasp, pulling away from him. "I can't do this."

"But we did this last night," he says, looking at me with confusion.

"And it was a mistake," I mutter.

"So that's why you ran away while I was asleep? I have to say, I wasn't too happy when I woke up alone. I'd had plans to start my morning by waking you up with my tongue between your legs," he growls.

My pussy clenches at his words, and my whole body heats up with desire. I want that, more than anything.

He reaches down, making the skirt of my dress ride up a little as he caresses my bare thigh.

"But why did you regret it, babygirl?" he asks, his voice so deep and husky that it sends a shiver down my spine. "Last night, you didn't know I was your dad's boss. I was just some random guy."

I cover my face with my hands, feeling it burn as shame washes over me. "And that was the problem," I wail. "You were a random guy. I gave my virginity to some random guy the first night I met him, and it was stupid of me. I rushed into it, and it was amazing, but I should have waited before giving my first time to someone."

The words rush from my mouth as if I have no control over them.

He moves his hand away from my thigh, and when I peek up at him through my fingers, he's wearing an odd expression.

"You were still a virgin before last night?" he asks, sounding confused.

Damn it. Now he's going to think there's something wrong with me. I nod my head, and wish I hadn't bumped into him again tonight after all.

But then he's pulling my hands away from my face and pinning them back against the wall, while his mouth comes crashing down on mine. I gasp against his lips before my body responds, kissing him back with a ferocious need that makes me forget about everything else.

Doing this with him is wrong. I know that now. But I can't bring myself to care when he makes me feel so damn good.

Chapter Four

Nathan:

Emily was a virgin.

That's the thought that keeps repeating itself over and over in my mind as I push her back against the wall and kiss her, devouring her mouth. I knew she'd been inexperienced, but I never would have imagined she was completely untouched.

And now, she's all mine.

Her soft curves mold perfectly against me as her hands slide around my waist and her tongue meets mine in a slow, sensual dance. She's still inexperienced, but that's part of the thrill. It means I get to show her everything.

"Do you have any idea what you do to me?" I growl, pulling away from the kiss just enough to speak.

She shakes her head, and I can see the uncertainty and hesitation in her eyes. She thinks she's done something wrong. Something stupid. And maybe she has, because leaving me in the middle of the night was not the smartest move, but she's not going to run away again this time.

"I thought about you all day," I confess. "Couldn't concentrate on a damn thing. Couldn't get your perfect little body out of my mind."

Her cheeks flush pink, and she bites her lip. Fuck, she's adorable.

"And now I know that nobody else has ever touched you before, or been inside you; I want you even fucking more. It's like you were made for me, babygirl."

I kiss her again, hard and possessive, and she whimpers into my mouth. She wants this just as much as I do, and I'm not going to let her get away again.

I'm the kind of man who always gets what he wants, and I want Emily.

She moans softly as I kiss her, and my cock strains against the front of my pants, desperate to be inside her. The sexy little minx is wriggling against me, her body begging for more, and I'm tempted to lift her dress and fuck her right here in the corridor, where anyone could walk past and see us. Then I'd send her back to her parents with my cum dripping out of her sweet little cunt as a reminder that she belongs to me now.

"Mr. Harding?" someone says from the end of the corridor, their voice uncertain.

I let out a frustrated growl against Emily's lips and reluctantly pull away from her, positioning myself in front of her to shield her from view.

Jesus fucking Christ. It's Richard. Of course it is. The guy is always following me around, his nose so far up my fucking ass that I'm surprised I can walk straight on any given day. He's looking for a promotion to the new senior management position that's come up, and he's become even more of a pain in the ass than usual lately.

"What is it?" I ask through gritted teeth.

He's looking behind me, no doubt trying to catch sight of the woman I'm with, but I take a step closer to the wall she's leaning against, blocking her with my much larger frame.

I don't understand why, but I don't want him gawking at my girl. Just the thought of it has my blood boiling, and it's taking all my willpower to keep myself in check.

"Hi, Mr. Harding," he says, finally looking at me. "I noticed that the servers you've hired are too slow at refilling the trays with food and drink, and thought maybe you'd like me to talk to them about it?"

God, he really is insufferable.

"I'm sure they are doing their best," I say, glaring at him. "There are a lot of people for them to serve, so just be patient with them, okay? They are a company I've used lots of times for events and I trust them to do a good job."

"Okay," he says, stretching his neck in his attempt to look past me. "So you don't want me to..."

"No," I snap, cutting him off. "There is no need for you to do anything, Richard. Just go back to the party and relax. Enjoy yourself. Have a few drinks."

"Yes, Mr. Harding. Of course."

He nods and starts backing away from us, not turning his back until he's practically around the corner. I roll my eyes, shaking my head.

"God, the guy is an idiot," I mutter.

Emily giggles and places a hand on my back, and that's enough to soothe me and remind me of what I'd been doing before such a rude interruption.

"Where were we, babygirl?" I ask, turning back to her.

She blushes and bites her lip; and god, she's so damn sexy.

"I should probably get back to my parents," she says. "They'll be looking for me."

I'm not ready to let her go, not when she's right here and looking like this, so I cup her cheek and force her gaze to meet mine.

"Not yet," I say in a firm voice, and the little whimpering sound that emerges from her makes my cock twitch. "Not until I've made you come so damn hard that your legs will still be shaking when I send you back to them."

Her eyes widen, and she looks nervous, but there is also a clear glimmer of arousal in her expression, and I know that she wants this as much as I do.

"Are you going to be a good girl for me?" I ask, running a finger along her jaw and down her throat.

"Yes," she whispers.

"That's my girl."

I crouch down in front of her, holding the front of her skirt up with one hand against her stomach, and tracing the fingers of my other hand along her slit. The little lace panties she's wearing are soaked, and I can't help but grin to myself.

"So nobody else has touched you here before last night?"

"No," she whispers, before hesitating. "Well, except..."

My eyes snap up to her face and my entire body tenses. Who am I going to have to destroy for touching my girl? I'd do it in an instant. Without hesitation or regret. The thought of another man touching what's mine is enough to make me want to commit murder.

"Except who?"

She hesitates for a long moment before speaking. "Except me, obviously," she says, her face flushed bright red.

Relief floods through me, just as images of her laid out on her bed, moaning and writhing as she fingers herself fill my mind. Fuck, that's hot.

"Okay," I say with a chuckle. "I don't mind that at all. And I already know nobody else has filled this sweet little pussy with cock. Only I have. But has anybody else ever kissed you here? Used their mouth on you to make you come?"

She shakes her head, and god, she's perfect. I pull the lace panties aside, and my mouth waters at the sight of her glistening wet folds.

"Well, that's going to have to change, babygirl. Because your pretty little cunt is begging to be devoured."

"Oh, god," she whimpers, her head falling back against the wall.

She's panting now, her chest rising and falling rapidly, and she looks so damn sexy that it takes all of my self-control not to take her right here, right now. But that's not how I want this to go tonight. I want to show her just how damn good I can make her feel, so she'll never want to run out on me again.

"You want me to eat your sweet little pussy?" I growl, tracing a finger along her slit and dipping inside her, just enough to coat my fingertip with her juices.

"Yes," she moans. "Please, Nathan."

"That's a good girl."

I pull my hands away and slip my fingers in the waistband of her panties, slowly pulling them down her legs. When she steps out of them,

I screw them up into a ball and tuck them into the pocket of my suit jacket.

They will be a nice souvenir for me to enjoy later, once everyone has gone home.

Then I'm pushing up her skirt once more, groaning softly as I see a drop of moisture leaking from between those mouth-watering folds, and I can't hold back any longer. I lean forward and press my lips against her pussy, groaning at how fucking delicious she tastes.

Her knees buckle, but I grip her hips firmly before she can fall, lifting one of her legs over my shoulder so she can balance herself. She gasps and whimpers as my tongue dives between her lips, lapping up her juices.

"Oh, god, Nathan. That feels... Oh!"

Her words trail off, and her hands fly down to tangle in my hair. I chuckle, the sound vibrating against her clit, and her legs begin to tremble. Her soft, wet flesh is quivering against my lips, and her sweet nectar is already leaking out to coat the lower half of my face.

"This is my pussy, isn't it, babygirl? Only I've fucked you, and only I've tasted you, and from now on, nobody else will ever touch you here except me. You're mine, Emily."

"Mmhmm," she whines.

I groan against her, sliding two fingers into her tight, wet pussy, while I bring my mouth back to her clit. I suck on the sensitive bud, flicking my tongue across it, and her moans grow louder and louder. Her grip on my hair tightens, and she's pulling me closer, pushing herself further onto my fingers; and goddamn, she's a fucking delight.

I pump my fingers in and out of her, faster and faster, curling them up to find her g-spot, while my tongue works her clit. She's moaning and crying out, her pussy tightening around my fingers as her whole body begins to tremble.

Perhaps I should be worried about all the noise she's making, in case someone hears and comes to find out what's going on. But I can't stop. She tastes so fucking good, and the noises she's making are intoxicating.

The feeling of her slick pussy around my fingers is addictive, reminding me of how amazing it had felt last night when those velvety walls had gripped my cock tightly. I'm lost in the taste of her, and the feeling of her body, and the way she's clinging onto me for dear life.

She's close. So damn close. And when she falls apart, it's going to be the most intense orgasm of her life. I'm going to make damn sure of that.

I pick up the pace, pumping my fingers in and out of her while I swirl my tongue around her clit. She's bucking her hips, working herself against my mouth and fingers, and her grip on my hair is painfully tight.

"Nathan!" she cries out, and a split second later, her whole body shudders as she comes hard.

Her legs are trembling violently, and her juices flood out of her, coating my hand and wrist. I keep moving my fingers, drawing out her pleasure, not stopping until the final waves of her orgasm have faded away.

When she lets out a contented sigh and releases her grip on my hair, I slowly remove my fingers and press one last kiss against her clit.

"Good girl," I say, lifting her leg off my shoulder and helping her to stand on both feet as I rise up to stand once more.

She's flushed and panting, her eyes slightly glazed, and it takes her a moment to focus on my face.

"Holy shit," she whispers. "That was... wow."

I laugh, brushing a stray strand of hair away from her face with two wet fingers.

"Good, I'm glad you enjoyed it, babygirl. And I'm only asking for one small thing in return."

She frowns, looking adorably confused. "What's that?"

I reach into my pocket and pull out my phone. With swift fingers, I open the menu and begin setting up a new contact before handing it to her.

"Your number. So I can make sure I've got a way to get hold of you, even if your doubts start getting the better of you again."

She huffs, but doesn't argue.

I grin as I watch her tap in her details and hand the phone back.

"Thanks, babygirl."

The way she smiles at me warms my heart, and I can't resist leaning in to kiss her again. My cock is aching, but I ignore the need. Tonight is her turn. It's my job to give her pleasure. So that when she goes back out into the party, she'll know that none of those men out there could ever please her as well as I can.

But I'll be claiming her tight little pussy again soon enough.

"I'll call you," I say, stepping away.

She blushes, looking flustered, and fuck, it's so damn cute.

"Go," I urge her, taking another step back. "I'll see you soon, babygirl."

She nods and hurries away, glancing over her shoulder at me with a shy smile before she disappears around the corner. I lean back against the wall and let out a deep sigh.

I can't believe she turned up at my house tonight. It's like fate is bringing us back together again. And now, there is no way I'm going to let her get away.

I don't care if she is the daughter of one of my employees.

She's mine.

Chapter Five

Emily:

I can't help but smile when I check my phone near the end of my lunch break on Sunday to find a text from Nathan. It's been impossible to hide the smile I've been wearing after bumping into him again last night. Mom and Dad had been wondering what had got into me when I'd rejoined them at the party, especially considering the sour mood I'd been in when we'd arrived, but luckily for me, they didn't ask too many questions.

It's not like I could tell Dad that his boss had just eaten my pussy and made me come so hard that I was still seeing stars. So it was definitely a good thing they didn't ask why I was suddenly grinning ear-to-ear.

And every time I'd glanced in Nathan's direction throughout the party, he had been watching me with the same intense look on his face that he'd had the first night we'd met. I have to admit, it's a bit of a thrill to have someone so powerful and successful chasing after me. I never would have imagined the guy I'd ended up giving my virginity to on a whim could be my dad's boss.

I unlock my phone screen and check the message.

Nathan: *I want to see you today. Are you busy?*

I grin and nibble my lip as an excited flutter appears in my belly and seems to spread through my entire body.

Me: *Sorry. I'm at work today, but I can text you after my shift.*

The little bubble appears straight away to show he's typing his reply, and I pace back and forth in the break room while I wait the few seconds it takes for his next message to appear.

Nathan: *Where do you work, babygirl?*

I don't know why it always creates a warm tingle in the pit of my stomach when he calls me that, but it does. He's so damn sexy, and it's difficult to wrap my mind around the fact that it's me he wants.

Me: *Tender Hearts Animal Shelter. I should finish about five. We can meet up then?*

Nathan: *I'll see you soon, Emily.*

I chuckle and slip my phone back in my bag before putting it in my locker. It's time to get back to work. But there's a bounce in my step and a smile on my face as I head out to the dog kennels, and I can't remember the last time I felt this happy.

"Hey, Emily!"

"Hi, Jasmine," I say with a bright smile, pausing when I see the shift supervisor. "Anything in particular you want me to do this afternoon?"

"Yeah, do you think you could spend some time with Benny? He really needs to get better at socializing if we want to find him a home, and you're the only one he will let anywhere near him. Do you mind?"

Benny the Bulldog was brought in three weeks ago by his previous owner's neighbors, who had found him tied up in the backyard. The owners had moved a few days before and had decided to leave the poor guy behind. It was obvious he'd been mistreated, and he has been wary of people ever since he arrived. But, for some reason, he has taken a liking to me, and so I have been spending extra time with him whenever I'm working.

"Of course," I say. "I'd love to. He's so damn adorable."

Jasmine smiles and pats me on the arm. "Thanks. I've got to go get a new arrival signed in and checked out by the vet, so have fun with Benny."

I head to the kennels and find him curled up in his cage, his big brown eyes following me as I approach.

"Hi, buddy," I say, crouching down.

After opening the cage, I hold out my hand and wait patiently for him to crawl towards me. The poor guy has been skittish around people, so I don't want to scare him off by rushing him. After a moment, he comes to me and nuzzles his nose against my fingers.

"Do you wanna play ball?" I ask, and he gives a soft woof of excitement.

I pull his favorite ball out of the pocket of my apron and hold it up.

"Okay, let's go!"

He jumps up and races after me, quickly getting in front of me, his eyes already locked on the ball in my hand.

"That's a cute dog," says a familiar voice, and I drop the toy in surprise.

Benny bounds towards it regardless and picks it up in his jaws.

"Nathan!" I gasp. "I feel like you keep showing up in unexpected places. What are you doing here?"

Nathan chuckles as he stands on the other side of the chain-link fence that surrounds the yard. He's dressed in a pair of jeans and a navy blue shirt that looks damn good on him. I try not to let my eyes linger too long, though, since the sight of him makes my stomach flip and my heart race.

"For the record, the last time I surprised you, you were in my house, so I believe you were the one in an unexpected place. Not me. And I told you that I wanted to see you today. I wasn't sure I could wait until five."

One corner of his lip curls upwards into a sexy smirk, and I have to admit I like that he's come looking for me.

"Fair point. Well, I guess you can join me and Benny, then."

I walk over to the gate, unlocking it for Nathan and opening it just enough for him to fit through while keeping an eye on the dog.

"Hey, boy," he says, lowering himself down into a crouch and holding out a hand in Benny's direction.

The dog is hesitant at first, but when Nathan doesn't move, and doesn't try to get closer, the dog begins to slowly creep forward, his eyes on Nathan's hand.

"That's it, good boy. I won't hurt you. That's a good boy," Nathan coos softly, and my heart melts a little.

It's impossible not to be attracted to a guy who's gentle with animals. Especially when he looks so damn good doing it.

"Be careful," I whisper. "Benny is a cutie pie with me, but he was mistreated by his owners. He's not too good with people."

Nathan nods, but remains still otherwise, allowing the dog to sniff around him for a few seconds. When he's finished, Benny walks away and flops down at my feet. I laugh and sit on the floor, scratching behind one of his ears.

"Good boy, Benny. That's a good boy."

"He really likes you, doesn't he?" Nathan asks, taking a seat beside me.

I can't help but blush when he shifts his body closer, his shoulder brushing against mine. I want to move even closer, maybe even close the gap between us completely and crawl into his lap, but I have a feeling I'd get into trouble for doing something like that at work.

"He's a sweetie," I reply.

"So are you."

I smile at his comment, and he grins back, making my heart flutter. But I guess now is as good a time as any to have the conversation that I need to have with Nathan. When I'm at work and he can't touch me in ways that make my brain fuzzy.

"I really enjoyed last night," I whisper. "But I don't know if this is a good idea. You're my dad's boss, and I know he'd go crazy if he found out about us."

Nathan's lips quirk up, and he chuckles softly.

"He might go crazy if he finds out, but you know what, babygirl? I really don't care."

My jaw drops, and I shake my head.

"What do you mean, you don't care?"

"I mean, I like you, and I knew from the moment I saw you that you're mine. The fact that your dad is one of my employees is irrelevant."

I swallow hard, trying to fight the blush creeping up my cheeks. I should have expected a man as confident and dominant as Nathan to be a little... possessive. There is a part of my brain telling me that I shouldn't like this kind of behavior. But there's a much larger part of my brain that is screaming the opposite. The part of me that is turned on by the thought of him wanting me. If he wants to possess me, I'm not sure I have the strength to tell him no.

Not when my heart wants him so badly. And that's not even taking into account the effect he has on my body whenever he's close.

"Dad won't get into trouble at work, will he?" I ask softly. "He won't lose his job or anything?"

Nathan turns to look at me, gripping my chin firmly between his thumb and forefinger to keep my eyes on his.

"You have my word, Emily, that nothing bad will happen to your dad because of us."

"Okay," I breathe, and the way he's looking at me sends a shiver down my spine.

I can't look away, even though I'm desperate to, and his gaze is so intense, so heated, that it makes me feel a little breathless.

"You need to understand that I always get what I want, babygirl. And I want you. It's going to take a lot more than your father to keep me away from you."

It takes me a moment to realize that the little whimpering sounds I can hear are actually coming from me. A flush creeps across my cheeks, and Nathan smirks, leaning in closer.

"And if that doesn't convince you, then maybe this will," he murmurs, his breath tickling my skin.

His hand is still on my face, but he slides it round to cup the back of my head, pulling me closer until his lips finally meet mine.

It's a soft kiss, a slow one, but somehow, it manages to be hotter than all the others put together. His tongue brushes along the seam of my lips, and I open up to him, letting him claim my mouth in the most sensual kiss I've ever experienced.

By the time he pulls back to look into my eyes once more, I'm breathless and flustered, and only the sound of Benny whining next to me because I've stopped his ear scritches brings me back to reality.

Oh god, I don't know what Nathan has done to me, but I'm starting to think there is no coming back.

"You're mine, Emily," he says in a firm voice that sounds almost like a growl. "And after your shift, I'm going to take you back to my place and make you scream my name so many fucking times that you won't be able to forget it."

I'm practically panting as I stare at him. He's so sexy, and his words are so hot. I want to feel him inside me again. I need to.

"Okay," I whimper, unable to find any more words. Nathan's confidence and possessiveness have turned my brain to mush.

His lips twitch, and he leans forward, pressing one last chaste kiss to my forehead.

"You carry on working, babygirl. You don't mind if I hang around for the rest of your shift, do you?"

I shake my head, dazed, and he chuckles as he stands up, taking a seat on the bench and watching as I return my attention to the dog.

It is hard to concentrate, though, when all I can think about is Nathan's promise to fuck me senseless later.

My thighs clench together, and I squirm a little.

God, I hope this shift goes quickly.

Chapter Six

Nathan:

I can't keep my eyes off Emily all afternoon as she continues working. And she seems to feel the same way about me. Every few seconds, she glances over, and her cheeks turn the most adorable shade of pink every time.

Fuck, the girl is driving me crazy.

I never imagined when I set my sights on her that she would have such an effect on me. I've never felt like this before, and I've certainly never spent an afternoon waiting around for a girl at her workplace, like a love-sick teenager.

But, despite everything, I don't regret it.

I have no idea what this is between us, or where we are headed, but there is something about her. Something that calls to me, that pulls me in and refuses to let go.

She's perfect, and she's mine.

It's not until five o'clock, when the few other staff begin filtering out, that I stand up and walk over to her.

"Are you ready to leave, babygirl?" I ask, reaching out and resting a hand on her hip.

"Yes," she breathes, her eyes wide, and a little dazed.

Fuck, she's cute.

I lean in, brushing my lips across hers, and she melts against me, her lips parting to give me access. I slide my tongue into her mouth, and she tastes so damn sweet.

A low growl rumbles from deep within my chest, and she whimpers softly, her fingers curling into the front of my shirt.

"Fuck, Emily, the things you do to me," I groan, breaking the kiss.

"I feel the same way about you," she replies, her cheeks flushing.

I smile and press another chaste kiss to her lips. "Now it's time for me to take you somewhere private so I can do all the filthy things to you that I've been imagining while watching you work."

Her blush deepens, and she bites her bottom lip, but she nods and takes a step back.

"I'll see you tomorrow, Jasmine," she calls out to an older woman as we walk past her on the way out.

"Have a good night, Emily. See you later," the woman calls back.

We head out of the shelter, and I slide an arm around Emily's waist.

"Where are you parked?" I ask.

"Oh, I don't have my car. I walked to work today."

"Good, I can drive us, then. We're going to my place."

It seems like the only option. I know from conversations I've had with Ted Walker that his one and only daughter still lives with him. And I can't imagine he'd be too happy if I turned up on his doorstep with Emily.

That's a conversation I will need to have with him another day because he's going to have to accept the fact she belongs to me. But right now, I just need to get my girl out of those clothes and underneath me.

I lead her to my car and open the passenger door for her, taking a moment to admire the way her jeans show off the curves of her ass perfectly. It looks almost good enough to eat.

"Come on, babygirl. We'll be there soon," I say, closing the door after her and heading around the front of the car.

The drive to my house is blissfully short, and I spend the whole time trying to keep my eyes on the road. But the fact she's sitting beside me, so close that her scent fills my senses and makes my cock ache, is too tempting.

So tempting that I consider parking the car and fucking her at the side of the road. But I'm six three, and my sports car isn't going to give me enough space to fuck her the way I want. No, I need to get her to the privacy of my home, and soon.

I park in my driveway and hurry around to open the door for Emily. She climbs out, and I take her hand, leading her into the house.

Usually, I would give her a grand tour, but she was at my house just last night. It looks different tonight, though, without all the party decorations and the crowds of people.

Tonight, it's just us.

Just the way I want it.

As soon as the front door is closed behind us, I slide an arm around Emily's waist, sweeping her feet up off the floor so she's forced to wrap her legs around my waist. The moan that escapes her causes my cock to twitch, and I can't stop myself from crashing my lips against hers.

I slam her back against the wall, my tongue diving into her mouth and claiming her. It's a desperate kiss, and it's exactly what I need. She's so responsive, clinging to me like she never wants me to let her go.

But I want more. I need more.

"I've got to have you, babygirl," I say, carrying her towards the stairs.

"Yes," she whimpers. "Please."

"I'm going to make you scream my name, Emily. Over and over."

I don't bother waiting for a reply, kissing her hard and swallowing the sounds of her moans. By the time we reach my room, her lips are red and swollen from our kisses.

I place her down on her feet, and without having to say a word, we both begin tugging at each other's clothes at the same time. Within moments, there's a pile of clothes at my feet and a beautiful naked woman standing in front of me.

Emily takes a step closer, and I swoop her up into my arms again. She's so fucking short I'm pretty sure I could carry her around in my pocket all day, and I love the feel of her little body pressing against mine as I carry her around. Her pussy traps my rock hard dick against my abs as she clamps her legs around my waist, and I can feel she's already dripping wet.

I carry her over to the bed and sit on the edge, keeping my arm firmly around her so she can't wriggle off my lap. My other hand slides between her thighs, and I run a finger through her slick folds.

"Who does this pretty little cunt belong to, babygirl?" I ask, my voice thick and deep with the overwhelming urge to claim her wet little hole again.

My words make her whimper, and her cheeks flush red.

"It belongs to you, Nathan," she whispers, and it's the hottest thing I've ever heard.

"Damn fucking right, it does," I growl. "I'm the only man who's ever touched you. Who's ever fucked you. And even the only man to taste you. It's all fucking mine, Emily."

As I say the final words, I slide two thick fingers straight inside her pussy, groaning as the tight inner muscles flutter around the digits. Her fingers are digging into my shoulders, her nails scraping along my skin, and I find myself hoping it will leave marks.

There's no better badge of honor than when a woman comes so hard she claws the hell out of her man.

"And do you want to know something else, Emily?" I ask.

Her only response is a nod of her head while she gasps and moans, bouncing a little on my fingers in her eagerness to be fucked.

God, how can anybody be this damn perfect?

"It's not just your pussy that's mine. All of you belongs to me, Emily."

I lean in closer, brushing my lips against the side of her neck before nipping at the pale flesh hard enough that it's bound to leave a little mark. And if I have my way, it won't be the only mark on her skin by the end of the night.

I'm not sure if it's my words or the sensation of my teeth grazing against the delicate flesh that makes her moan, but either way, I want to hear more.

"Oh, Nathan," she whimpers. "I don't understand why I feel so drawn to you. I shouldn't. You're my dad's boss. But I can't resist you."

I reach up and grab a fistful of her hair, tugging it just hard enough that her heavy-lidded eyes open wide. She stares up at me, panting with the intensity of her desire.

"That's because you know just as well as I do that you belong with me. You feel it too. There's no reason to fight it, babygirl. You and I are meant to be. If that wasn't the case, you would have given your virginity to one of the many boys I suspect you had chasing around after you. Instead, you waited for me, even though, at the time, I was only some stranger you met in a bar."

The pretty flush of her cheeks is all the evidence I need that I'm right.

I slide my fingers out of her, and the needy little whining noise she makes at suddenly being empty is like music to my fucking ears.

"Slide down on my cock, babygirl," I growl, something animalistic taking over now. "Ride my dick and make yourself come on it. Show me that this is the only cock you'll ever want from now on."

I'm so fucking hard it hurts, and the only thing that's going to ease that is her perfect little cunt.

"Yes, Sir," she breathes, a hint of a smile playing at her lips.

Fuck.

Sir.

I don't think there's a word in the English language that's sexier than that coming from her. I hear it multiple times a day from my employees, but when she says it, it's like a whole new word.

And it's fucking hot.

Emily shifts, moving her knees further apart, and I hold the base of my cock steady so she can line up with it. Her head drops back and a loud moan escapes her as her heat covers me, her pussy slowly sliding down the full length of my dick.

"Nathan, oh god," she cries, her voice sounding so desperate. "You're so big. It feels so good."

Her hips roll, and a groan rumbles deep in my chest. Her wet little cunt is dripping wet, and so tight it's got me in a fucking chokehold. It's almost painful, but in the best way possible.

I want to stay here, just like this, forever.

Emily starts riding me, bouncing up and down on my cock, and I lie back on the bed, glancing up at the beauty above me. Her tits jiggle with each movement, and I can't resist reaching up and cupping them in my hands.

"Get ready, babygirl," I warn. "I'm about to fuck you so hard you won't be able to walk for a week."

And that's all the warning she gets before I grip her hips, digging my fingers into the soft flesh, and start pounding up into her. Her moans are loud and uncontrollable, and each sound sends a fresh surge of blood to my cock.

I can't even remember the last time I was this turned on.

It's never been like this. Not with anyone.

And when she starts trembling, her cunt tightening around me, I can tell she's close to her orgasm. I want to come with her. Need to.

I need to fill her pussy and make her mine.

"That's it, babygirl. come on my cock and scream my name," I growl.

"Nathan," she cries. "Oh god, Nathan."

The feeling of her walls clenching around my length is too much, and I thrust hard and fast, driving her up towards her peak. And then her cunt is spasming around me, milking my cock, and my vision blurs for a moment as my own orgasm slams into me.

"Fuuuuck, Emily," I growl, gripping her hips tight and holding her still as I shoot load after load of cum deep inside her.

She collapses on top of me, her panting breaths warming my skin, and I slide my arms around her, hugging her tight.

"Oh, Nathan," she breathes.

"Yes, babygirl," I reply, kissing the side of her head.

"That was incredible."

"Yes, it was."

She giggles, the sweet sound sending a wave of warmth through me.

I know she has no idea what this is, and to be honest, I don't really either. All I know is that I want her. She's mine, and there's nothing that can change that.

Emily tenses in my arms, and before I can react to the sensation, she moves into a sitting position, her face pale except for the glow on her cheeks from the previous exertion.

"Oh god," she says, panic lacing her words. "We didn't use protection, Nathan. And we didn't use it last time. Oh god, I didn't even think about it. I'm so stupid."

I push myself up into a sitting position and pull her into my arms. "You are not stupid," I say firmly. "I did think about it, and I decided it wasn't necessary. You are mine, and I will take care of you no matter what happens. You and all the babies I plan to put inside you."

A grin tugs at the corners of my lips, and her eyes widen in shock. I don't miss the little whimper that escapes her before she can clamp her lips shut, though.

I chuckle and lean forward, brushing my lips against hers. "And if you're lucky, I might even fill you up with another load of my cum before I take you home tonight, babygirl."

"Oh, Nathan," she moans, as her body melts and her lips crash against mine.

I cup the back of her head, returning her kiss and pulling her closer. She feels so fucking good against me, and her lips are addictive. I can't get enough of them.

Of her.

And judging by her reaction when I told her I plan to knock her up, she's given up on the idea of trying to resist the feelings between us.

Because she knows just as well as I do.

We're meant to be together.

She belongs to me.

Chapter Seven

Emily:

I'm practically floating on air during the short walk to my parents' house. Nathan had, of course, insisted on driving me home, seeing as it was dark by the time we'd finally left his house. But I'd asked him to park down the block a little so my dad wouldn't see me climbing out of his boss's car. Or see the goodbye kiss that lingered far too long and left both Nathan and I feeling more than a little heated. For a moment, I'd suspected he was going to start the car and take me back to his house again for another round, but he'd reluctantly let me go when I'd told him I didn't want to stay out much later otherwise Mom and Dad might start wondering where I am.

I have to admit I was worried how he'd take that news. After all, he's a forty-nine-year-old man who also happens to be incredibly successful. He doesn't answer to anybody but himself. Meanwhile, I'm twenty-one, and still living with my slightly over-bearing parents. But he hadn't batted an eyelid. Instead, he'd kissed me softly and told me to text him once I'm inside so he knows I'm safe.

It's not like I can't take care of myself, but it's a really sweet gesture, and it makes my heart flutter to know he cares about me so much already.

As I approach the house, I see the living room light on and mutter a few curse words under my breath. It's past midnight, and my parents are usually in bed by ten. Well, my dad goes to sleep at that time, and Mom usually reads in bed until she's ready to settle for the night, too. And I know it's because she likes to listen out for me and make sure I get home safely.

So what's going on tonight that means Dad felt the need to stay up until I got home?

I ignore the heavy feeling in my chest as I slip into the house through the front door. Once I'm inside, I shoot off a quick text to Nathan to let him know I'm safe, so I can focus on whatever is going on with my parents without him worrying about me.

But when I look up from my phone, I notice my mom and dad have come out to greet me by the front door. And neither of them look happy.

Especially my dad.

Shit.

"Where have you been?" he asks through gritted teeth.

"I was at a friend's house," I answer quickly.

It's not exactly a lie. Nathan is a friend. He just also happens to be a lot more than that, too.

Dad narrows his eyes, staring at me intently, and I try my best not to fidget.

"A friend's house?" he repeats, and judging by the tone of his voice, he doesn't believe me. "So you weren't with Mr. Harding, then?"

He spits those final words out, and I flinch. How the hell could he know?

I open my mouth, but when I can't find anything to say that wouldn't make this situation exponentially worse, I close it again.

"I had a phone call today while you were at work, from one of my colleagues," he says, taking a step closer. Mom remains in the background, looking at me with an expression that lets me know just how disappointed she is with me.

"He told me that he saw you with my boss last night," Dad continues. "He said that the two of you were hiding away together in a dark hallway, and that the scene looked very intimate. Is something going on between you and Mr. Harding, Emily?"

Damn it. That Richard guy who interrupted us must have snitched to Dad about it.

Dick by name, dick by nature, I guess.

"He said he knew it was you because he saw you with us later in the evening and he recognized the dress you were wearing," Mom adds in a softer voice.

Well, there goes my chance to try to insist it was someone else.

"Look, it's not what you think, Dad," I say, hating the way my voice sounds so shaky.

"It's not?" he asks. "Well, that's good. Because I've spent all day thinking that maybe my daughter is fucking my boss."

I flinch again at his words and at the vitriol in his tone. Dad's face is bright red, and he takes another step forward, closing the gap between us.

"Tell me I'm wrong, Emily," he says, and the tone of his voice is terrifying.

I don't think I've ever seen him this angry before.

"Dad, I swear I didn't know he was your boss when I first met him. And then when I did find out, I couldn't help it. I really like him, Dad. He's kind, and he treats me well."

"Oh, god," he mutters, turning his back on me and pacing across the room. "You are sleeping with him. How could you, Emily? He's twice your age."

"So?" I answer, feeling the frustration rising up inside me. "What has that got to do with anything when it feels so right?"

"You are a child, Emily," Dad snaps. "How can you think any of this is okay? I can't believe you would disrespect me so much."

"I'm twenty-one, Dad," I say, fighting back the tears that sting the corners of my eyes. "I'm an adult, and I can date whoever I like. I know he's your boss, and that might feel a bit awkward, but I really like him. He makes me so happy."

"Happy?" Dad says, the disbelief dripping from his words. "You're being ridiculous, Emily. You won't see him anymore."

I shake my head. "No. You can't make me stop seeing him."

"Actually, I can," he answers, and the coldness in his voice sends a shiver down my spine. "As long as you are living under my roof, you will obey my rules, young lady. So I want you to call him and put an end to this. And I just have to hope your foolishness hasn't cost me my job.

God, I so wanted that damn promotion, and I can't believe you are stupid enough to risk this all for me, Emily."

"Dad, please. Don't do this," I plead.

I can't lose Nathan.

With a trembling hand, I swipe away the tears that are now spilling down my cheeks.

"You have a choice, Emily. You can either stay here and obey my rules, or you can pack your things and get the hell out of my house."

My heart skips a beat, and my mouth drops open in shock.

I can't believe he would really kick me out just because I'm seeing Nathan.

I can't believe any of this is happening.

"Well, what's it going to be?" he snaps.

"Fine," I say. "I'll leave."

"Good. Pack your things and go. Now."

And with that, he turns and walks away, leaving me standing in the hallway, shaking and crying and not entirely sure what just happened.

Mom doesn't say a word, and a few moments later, I hear her footsteps as she follows Dad. I can't believe she didn't try to stand up for me. If anyone can calm my dad down when he's being irrational, it's Mom. I must have really fucked up if she agrees with him.

I run up the stairs to my bedroom, filled with shame and guilt, and start throwing clothes into the suitcase that usually lives in the bottom of my wardrobe. But the tears are blurring my vision and making it hard to see.

I'd known they would be mad, but I hadn't thought they would throw me out over this.

It's not fair. They can't make me stop seeing the man I'm falling in love with.

By the time I'm ready to leave, I've stopped crying, and I've made a decision. I'm going to Nathan's.

I can't let this be the end for us.

I pull my suitcase down the stairs, and when I reach the hallway, I see Mom and Dad are still there. They're watching me silently, and my dad's arms are crossed over his chest.

"Please don't do this, Emily," Mom says. "Please, take some time to think about this. Is he really so important to you that he's worth leaving your family for?"

"I don't want to leave," I answer between sniffles. "But Dad isn't giving me any choice. I think I love Nathan, and I want to be with him. And if I can't do that while still living here, then I will have to go."

Mom looks at Dad, her eyebrows raised.

"She's made her choice," he says gruffly, not taking his eyes off me.

I give Mom a sad smile, and she sighs.

"I love you, baby," she whispers.

"I love you, too," I reply. "And I'm sorry."

With a heavy heart, I pull open the door and step outside. The night air is chilly, much cooler than it had been earlier in the day, and I hug my coat tighter around my body as I pull my suitcase towards my car that's sitting in the driveway.

When I turn back to look at the house, the front door is shut, and the house is in darkness.

They didn't even wait for me to leave.

I blink the tears from my eyes and get into my car, setting off in the direction of Nathan's house.

Chapter Eight

Nathan:

I take a sip of my scotch, then place the glass down on the table beside my armchair. It's late, but I'm not ready to sleep yet. My mind is too full of Emily and the many ways I want to claim all her pretty little holes.

Despite fucking her three times this evening, my cock hardens instantly at the thought of her. I reach down and readjust myself in my pants, letting out a little grunt as my hand lingers longer than I'd intended, giving my shaft a gentle squeeze.

Just as I'm considering pulling out my dick and giving myself some relief before bed, I'm disturbed by a knock on the front door. I glance at the clock and see that it's just past one in the morning. Who the fuck is calling on me at this time?

I groan and stand up, heading through the house and to the front door. When I swing it open, the sight before me fills me with both joy and concern.

Emily is standing there, dressed in the same outfit she'd been wearing when I dropped her home, a single suitcase by her side and her face streaked with tears.

"Nathan," she cries, and then she's throwing herself into my arms, sobbing uncontrollably.

"Hey, hey," I say gently, sliding my arms around her and hugging her tight. "What's the matter, babygirl? What happened?"

I guide her into the house, bringing the suitcase with me, and close the door, keeping my arm around her shoulders.

"I'm so sorry to just turn up like this," she sobs, "but I didn't know where else to go. My dad found out about us and he told me I either had to get out of his house or leave you."

My blood runs cold, and my mind starts running through all the possible ways Ted could have found out about us. Damn it. If it was that fucker, Richard, he'll be finding himself without a damn job tomorrow.

And what kind of fucking father kicks out his own daughter? It shouldn't matter who she is seeing.

Emily sniffles and her hands tangle in the front of my shirt, bringing me back to the present moment. I scoop her up in my arms and carry her through to the living room, settling in the armchair with her in my lap.

"It's okay, babygirl," I say, pushing down the anger inside me as I stroke her hair back from her face and focus on the only person who matters right now. "I will fix this, okay? I promise."

"I don't want to leave you, Nathan," she says, her voice coming out like a wail as she begins sobbing again. "But I don't want my dad to hate me either. I love you both, and I don't want to lose either of you."

My hand stills in her silken locks. She loves me? I have to fight back a grin, knowing now isn't the right time to look like a smug bastard. My girl needs comfort.

I lean in and press a gentle kiss to her forehead. "You won't lose either of us, Emily. I will talk to your dad tomorrow at work, and I'll straighten this all out. You have my word on that."

I'll give the fucker the promotion if that's what it takes to bring him round to the idea of me dating his daughter. Along with a raise far bigger than the one he would have got with the new job role alone. I'll pay whatever it fucking takes to buy back his favor just to put a smile on my girl's face again.

"And tonight," I continue, "you are staying right here, with me. You don't need to worry about anything, babygirl. Everything is going to be just fine."

"Really?" she asks, her voice coming out soft and shaky, and my heart breaks a little at the vulnerability in her tone.

"Really, Emily. Trust me."

She nods, and I hold her close as she nuzzles into my chest, letting her take comfort from my strength after such an emotional night.

I stand, holding her in my arms, still, carrying her like a bride across the threshold into the start of our new life together. I head upstairs and set her down on the edge of the bed, stripping her gently and pulling the covers over her before I undress and join her, wrapping my arms around her. The whole time, she has a soft smile on her lips, and her eyes never leave my face.

Tomorrow, I'll deal with her father. Tonight, I'm taking care of my precious babygirl.

"I love you too, Emily," I whisper, remembering her earlier confession and wondering if she even realizes she said it during her outburst.

Even in the darkness of my bedroom, I see the way her face lights up as I say those words. Her fingertips brush gently against my cheek, and I can't resist leaning forward and kissing her.

The kiss starts gentle and sweet, but the desire and passion soon consumes us. And when she begins wriggling against me, her little whimpers falling against my lips, I feel my resolve to just hold her and comfort her slip away.

"Aren't you tired, babygirl?" I ask her, and she shakes her head.

"I'm too wired to sleep," she replies. "But maybe we could..."

She bites her lip and a blush rises to her cheeks, making her look so sweet and innocent.

"Maybe we could what, babygirl?"

"I need you, Sir," she says, the words coming out as a plea, and fuck, I can't deny her when she looks at me like that.

"Okay, babygirl," I say, reaching between us and stroking the pad of my thumb over her clit. "Whatever you need, Emily."

She's soaking wet for me already, and I dip a finger into her slick channel, pumping it slowly in and out. She moans and bucks her hips, her eyes falling closed as she enjoys the sensation.

I continue fingering her for a while, enjoying the way she reacts to my touch. She's so sensitive and responsive, and her every reaction has my cock swelling against her.

When I can't wait any longer, I roll her onto her back, pulling her legs around my waist. My tip teases her entrance, and her eyes meet mine, looking at me with that same look of utter devotion.

I can't believe how lucky I am.

With one firm thrust, I'm inside her, and she gasps, her body arching up into me as I fill her.

I take her slowly, and the love in the air is so palpable, it's almost intoxicating. I can't remember ever being so consumed by someone before, and I can't help thinking that perhaps I've been waiting for this moment my entire life.

It's as though all the pieces of my life have finally slotted into place, and my world feels complete.

If her father thinks I'll let him take this away from me, he has another thing coming.

Emily is mine, and I will never let her go.

I slide in and out of her slowly, moaning as her tight inner walls grip my shaft so perfectly it's like she was made for me.

"Nathan," she whispers, and I lean down and press a kiss to her lips.

"I'm here, babygirl," I whisper, my pace speeding up as I feel my balls tighten, her impending release driving me closer and closer to the edge.

What started off as gentle love-making becomes a frantic fuck, both of us growing desperate for the pleasure we give each other. I buck my hips, thrusting into her wet and willing body as deep as I can go, enjoying the way she cries out each time I fill her completely.

"Oh god," she breathes. "Nathan, I... I'm going to..."

"Yes," I hiss. "Come for me, babygirl. Let me feel you."

I drive into her once more, and her pussy clenches around my cock, pulsing as she comes, her release spurring on my own.

With a moan, I hold my cock inside her, my seed shooting out and filling her, marking her as mine.

"Oh, god, yes," she whimpers, and her eyes fall closed, a satisfied smile spreading across her face.

"You're perfect," I tell her, my voice low and filled with awe.

I can't believe she's actually mine.

When we've both recovered, I pull out of her and roll onto my back, pulling her on top of me. She rests her head against my chest, and I run my fingers through her hair.

"It's going to be okay," I say, and she nods.

"I trust you," she whispers, and those three little words are all I need to hear.

As she drifts off to sleep in my arms, I vow that I will make everything right again.

I'll fix things with her dad and then I'll give her the world. My babygirl will never want for a single thing so long as I'm alive to take care of her.

Chapter Nine

Emily:

I can barely concentrate on grooming the new Labrador puppy that arrived at the shelter earlier today as a million worries swirl around in my mind.

What is Nathan going to say to Dad? And how will Dad take it?

Anxiety gnaws at my stomach. God, I hope things don't blow up between them. The last thing I want is for Dad to lose his job because of me.

I try to focus on running the brush through Dexter's fur, giving him a scratch under the chin with my free hand. He's a happy little guy, his tongue lolling out of the side of his mouth as he pants and enjoys all the attention.

He's only a few months old, and Golden Labradors always get adopted quickly from the shelter. I have no doubt he'll have a new home soon.

Unlike Benny. With his problems socializing, I expect it will take a lot longer to find a family who will want him.

I make a mental note to go and spend some time with him once I've finished with Dexter, and as soon as I'm done brushing the pup, I take him back to the kennels.

"There we go, boy," I say, placing him back in the cage and giving him a little treat. "That wasn't so bad, was it?"

He barks happily, and I grin, giving him a scratch behind the ear before closing the door to his cage.

I glance at the clock, and I realize that it's only a little over an hour before the end of the day. God, I can't wait to see Nathan again. Despite everything that's going on at the moment, it had felt amazing to spend the entire night in his bed, wrapped up in his arms.

The heavy feeling in the pit of my stomach lifts a little as thoughts of Nathan fill my mind. Everything will work out okay. I just know it will. He promised me he would take care of it, and he'd sounded so determined that it's difficult to imagine any outcome other than him fixing this mess.

I head towards Benny's cage, and I'm surprised to see Jasmine with him already. He's curled up in one corner, watching my supervisor with weary eyes, but he's not trembling, so I guess that's some kind of progress.

"Hey, Emily," she says with a smile as she notices me approaching. "You'll never guess what. Someone has signed the adoption papers for Benny and he'll be going to his new home soon. His new owner should be arriving any minute now."

My eyebrows raise in surprise. He's getting adopted?

"Are you sure he's ready for that?" I ask, feeling another fresh wave of worry creep over me. "I mean, I haven't even seen anyone here visiting with him. Shouldn't we give Benny a chance to get used to whoever is taking him home?"

Jasmine chuckles and looks me up and down, and it's only then I realize that I've moved to stand between her and the cage, my hands on my hips.

"Emily, I appreciate your concern, but we don't have the resources to keep a dog here indefinitely. He's already been here five months, and it's time we found him a home. I don't think this is a good environment for him when he's so nervous. I'm sure he'll start thriving once he's in a loving home."

Letting out a sigh, I have to admit to myself that she's right. I don't know why I feel this way about Benny. I've never had trouble letting go of one of the animals before. But he's different. I've bonded with him, and the idea of him not being here every day when I come to work makes me sad.

I can't be selfish, though. If a new home is what's best for Benny, then that's what I want for him.

The door to the kennel area opens, and another one of our co-workers, Irene, walks in.

"Benny's new owner is here," she says to Jasmine. "Is he ready?"

"Yep," Jasmine replies. "Can you tell them we'll be right out?"

Irene nods her head and disappears again.

She flashes me a sympathetic smile. "Would you like to be the one to take Benny out to his owner?" she asks in a soft voice.

Blinking back tears, I nod my head. It won't be easy, but at least I'll get to say goodbye and be the one to send him off to his new home.

Jasmine hands me a leash, and I take it from her, opening the cage door and clipping it to his collar.

"Come on, boy," I say, my voice a little more shaky than I would like it to be.

He follows me, making sure to swerve away from Jasmine as he walks past her, leaving a sizeable gap between them. I let out a small sigh. He's not going to be happy with anybody else. I'm the only person he feels safe with.

If it wasn't for the fact that I don't have a home of my own, I would be refusing to let him go and taking him home with me.

With heavy steps, I lead Benny out to the waiting area. But I come to an abrupt standstill in the doorway when I see who is sitting there.

"Nathan?" I ask, my heart racing as his face lights up. "What are you doing here?"

He's still in his suit, after coming straight here from work, no doubt.

"I wanted to surprise you, babygirl," he says. "I'm here to take you both home."

"Home?"

"Home," he confirms.

"Benny is coming to live with us?" I ask, and his beaming smile is enough to answer the question for me.

"Yes," he replies. "What do you say, babygirl? Do you and Benny want to move in with me?"

I squeal loudly, remembering a moment too late about Benny's sensitivity to noise when I see him flinch out of the corner of my eye.

"Yes!" I answer quickly, even as I crouch down beside my new pet and give him comforting head pats. "Oh my god. I can't believe this. Are you serious, Nathan?"

I glance up at him, his form blurry through the happy tears in my eyes.

"Completely," he replies. "As soon as I saw the two of you together yesterday, I knew Benny belonged with you. And I already know you belong with me. It makes sense that I should take you both home with me."

He looks down at me, a crooked grin on his lips that somehow manages to make him look even more handsome.

"If that's what you want, babygirl," he adds.

"Yes," I say, a sob catching in my throat even as a wide smile spreads across my face. "Yes, I want that more than anything."

Nathan's eyes soften, and he reaches out, helping me up to my feet and pulling me into his arms.

Happiness unlike anything I've ever felt before wells up inside me and I cling to Nathan tightly.

"Wait," I say, pulling back far enough to look into his eyes as a thought occurs to me. "Does that mean the talk with Dad didn't go well today? He still doesn't want anything to do with me?"

Nathan chuckles and presses a kiss to the tip of my nose. "No, Emily. It's nothing like that. The talk with your dad went really well, and I've even invited your parents to my place for dinner tomorrow night. And your dad accepted the invitation. But after last night, I've got no intention of going to sleep without you in my arms ever again."

His words make me melt inside, and my smile widens further. "I loved sleeping in your arms like that, Nathan. But what did you say to my dad to change his mind?"

A sheepish expression appears on his face. "Well, I started off by telling him how crazy I am about you, and how I plan to take such good care of you for the rest of our lives. Then I offered him the promotion to

Senior Manager, along with a very nice raise. And now he's the happiest man on the planet."

I laugh and roll my eyes. "Why doesn't that surprise me? Oh well, at least things are okay with him now."

"Let's go, babygirl. You can call your dad and chat to him about it while I drive us all, and then when we get home, we can celebrate the fact that you're moving in by christening every single room."

"Oh, my," I say, feeling a blush rising up my face.

But inside, the thought of what he's suggesting has butterflies fluttering around in my stomach and heat pooling between my legs.

"That sounds wonderful," I tell him.

"Good," he says, grabbing my hand.

We walk out the door together, Benny following behind, his tail wagging as though he can sense the happiness that's surrounding us.

I feel like the luckiest woman in the world.

I can't wait to spend the rest of my life with this man.

Epilogue

Emily:

Five months later:

"There you are," says Nathan as I walk through the front door of our home, Benny's leash in hand. "I've been missing you."

I grin and unclip the dog's leash, hanging it on a hook by the coat rack, then I rush to Nathan. Benny walks into the living room and flops down onto his plush dog bed, rolling over onto his back with his feet in the air, apparently ready for a nap after his run around at the dog park.

"I wasn't gone that long," I say with a giggle. "I was just taking Benny for a walk."

Nathan grins, a wicked quirk of the lips that promises many filthy things in my foreseeable future. "I know. But that doesn't mean I didn't miss you."

He lifts me easily in his arms and takes a few steps until my back is against the wall. I let out a whimper and wrap my arms and legs around him, but he's in the mood to take charge tonight. He tugs my arms away from his neck and then pushes them above my head, gripping my wrists firmly in one of his large hands.

It always makes me feel extra tingly when he's in this kind of mood. Letting him take control and do whatever he wants to me is one of my favorite things.

He presses a firm kiss to my lips, his tongue demanding entrance, and I open my mouth for him. Our tongues meet, and he devours me, his kiss deep and dominating.

At the same time, his free hand trails lower, his fingertips brushing against the slight swell of my belly. The bump is only just beginning to show, and it's not even big enough yet for people to know whether I'm pregnant or if I've just been eating a bit too much cake, but Nathan can never seem to keep his hands off it.

Even though it's only the third month of our pregnancy, neither of us can wait for our first child to be born.

Both my parents had been thrilled when we announced the news, and it's almost as if the fight between us never happened on the day they found out about Nathan and I. Now my Dad seems to be ridiculously proud that the CEO of the company he works for is his future son-in-law.

Nathan pulls his lips from mine and trails kisses down to my neck, nipping at the sensitive skin there to bring me back to the present moment.

I moan and wriggle against him as much as I can with the way he has me trapped helplessly against the wall. His erection presses against my pussy through our layers of clothing, and suddenly all I can think of is how badly I need him inside me.

"Please," I whimper, and I hear him chuckle.

"Please what, babygirl?" he asks, and the tone of his voice tells me he already knows what I want.

"Fuck me, please. I need it."

He grinds his cock against me and nips my neck again.

"So desperate," he says, and I whine.

He loves drawing this out and teasing me.

"Nathan, please."

He laughs, but finally gives in, releasing his hold on my wrists so he can slide his hands up under my skirt and tug my panties to the side. With a few swift movements, his cock is free, and then he's pushing it inside me.

I let out a gasp and arch my back, throwing my head back against the wall and enjoying the sensations as he starts to fuck me.

He's a perfect mix of rough and gentle, always holding back just enough to make sure he isn't hurting me.

The sound of our breathing and the slapping of our skin echoes through the hallway. Nathan pounds into me relentlessly, and it doesn't take long for the familiar tightening sensation to appear in the pit of my stomach. The feeling builds and grows until a release of pure pleasure explodes out of me.

My body shudders, and my walls clench around Nathan's cock as he continues to fuck me.

Moments later, I feel his own release. His hot cum spurts into me and his fingers dig into my hips. He groans my name as he finishes, and I wrap my arms and legs around him.

We stand together for a minute, both of us panting heavily as we come down from the high of our orgasms. But he doesn't let me down, and his still semi-hard cock remains buried inside me.

"I'm so happy you're mine, Emily," he says, his voice rough with emotion.

"Me too," I reply.

It's a sentiment we repeat often, and we're both as obsessed with each other as we were at the beginning.

Our love only grows stronger with every passing day.

And I can't wait to see what the future holds for us.

I already know it will be magical.

About The Author

Willow Watkins is a British author who has been obsessed with reading romances ever since she was a teenager. This love of reading has blossomed into an addiction to crafting her own love stories. Very spicy love stories, of course. Things always taste better with a bit of spice added, don't you think?

If you'd like to stalk her online, check out the following link: **https://allmylinks.com/willow-watkins**